LILA

01.02.2018

James V. Olenp

It started with an
"OOPS!"

and a
"LOOK OUT!"

and a
CRASH!

Then in walked Father Giant
with his quivering moustache.

"Who smashed my favourite elephant?"
he thundered through the door,
staring at the broken pieces
scattered
on
the
floor.

"When I find out *who* did this
I *will* punish them for sure,
with punishments more horrible
than any seen before.

"I'll make them find each tiny piece
and glue it back together,
and then I'll make them pack their bags
and leave this house

FOREVER."

Young Olive and her brother, Grub,
were hiding in a cupboard,
and when they heard the giant roar
they knew they'd been discovered.

"I see you hiding under there,
young Olive and young Grub,
so come out NOW, put up your hands,
explain this wild hubbub."

"I didn't mean to, honestly,"
said Grub, "it's not my fault.
I bumped my knee by accident
and did a somersault."

"I see, I see, so you're the one
who started all this mess,
with your bumping and your jumping
and your grubby clumsiness."

"No, no," said Grub, "I had to jump,
to catch the flying newt.
She leapt out of her fish tank
and forgot her parachute."

"Aha, I see, so Newt, it's you
who started all this mess,
with your splishing and your sploshing
and your naughty newtiness."

"Oh no, not I," the newt replied,
and wiggling her ear,
she pointed to the lady
in the crystal chandelier.

"I think you'll find the golden boot
that kicked me from the water
was dropped by Lady Ha-Ha, yes,
the Earl of Chortle's daughter."

"I see, so Lady Ha-Ha,
you're the cause of all this mess,
with your shrieking and your laughing
and your awful naughtiness."

"Oh no, not I," the lady cried,
"I didn't drop the boot.
It fell off quite by accident;
my goodness, what a hoot.

"I was riding through the forest
in this painting on the wall,
when Silly-Yak here bucked me off –
it makes no sense at all."

"Aha, I see, so Silly-Yak,
you started all this mess,
with your clipping and your clopping
and your yucky yakkiness."

"Oh no," said Yak, "it wasn't me,
I'd never do that, ever.
Myself and Lady Ha-Ha
we've been best of friends forever."

"We were walking
through the forest
when I heard
a sudden sound –
the sound of
Sophie Sofa shouting
'OOOOH'
and
'EEE'
and
OW'."

"Aha, so Sophie Sofa,
you're the one who scared the yak.
You'd better go and pack your bags,
you're never coming back."

"Oh why, no please, it wasn't me,"
the sofa stamped her feet.
"I only yelled a little yell
and that was from the heat.

"The sun came rolling down the hill
and landed in my lap,
all burning wet and soaking hot –
he woke me from my nap."

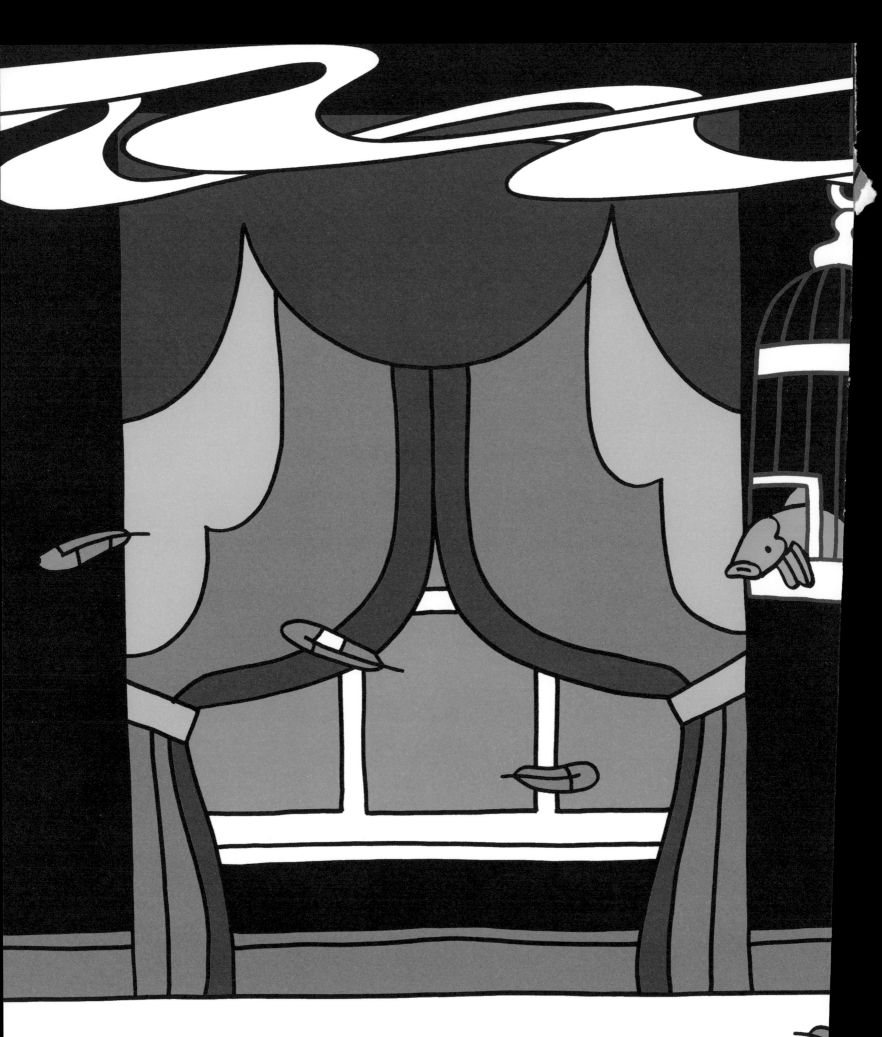

"Aha, so Sun," the giant said,
"you started all this mess,

"with your hissing and your smoking
and your funny sunniness."

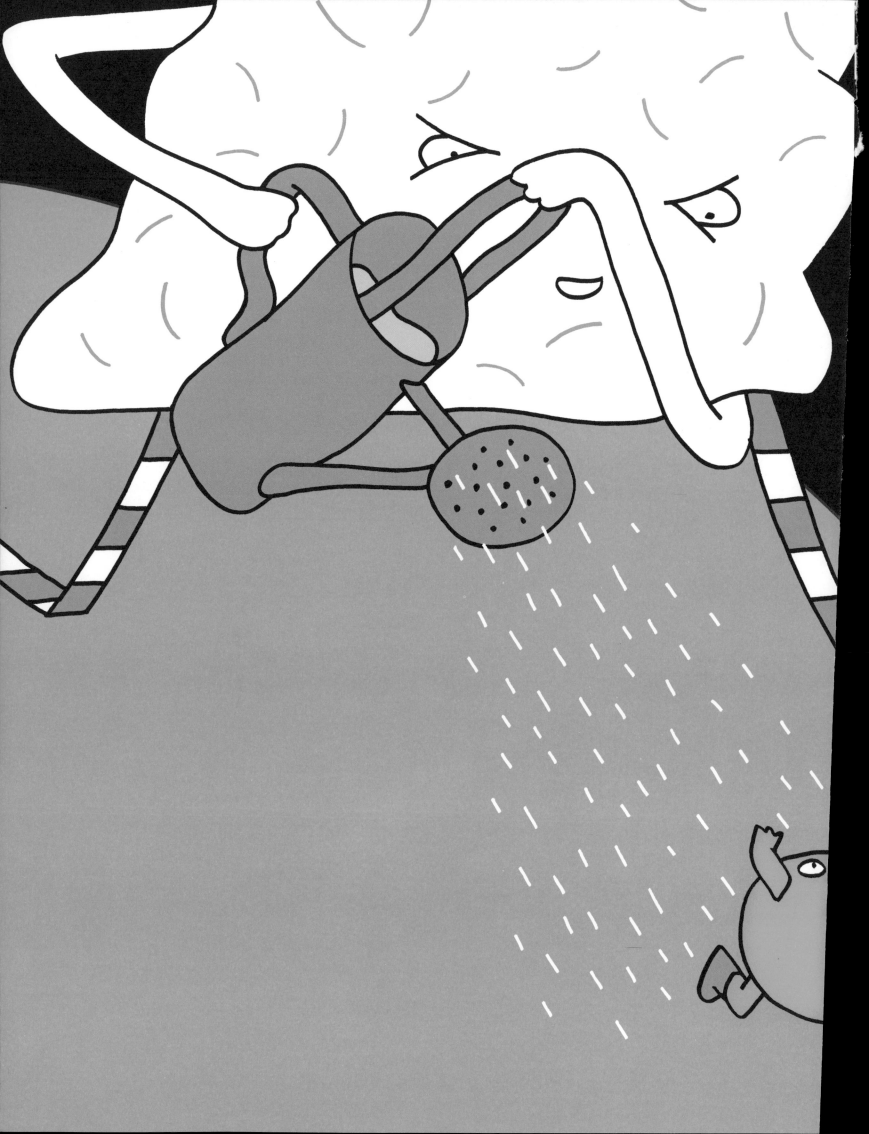

"Oh no," said Sun, "it *wasn't* me.
I like to play outside,
but nasty Storm *was* chasing me.
I ran in here to hide."

"Aha, I see, so nasty Storm,
you started all this mess,
with your whirling and your howling
and your rowdy cloudiness."

"Yes, yes," said Grub.
"That's right, the storm,
he chased the sopping sun,
who sat down on the sofa
with his red and fiery bum.
The sofa yelled a little yell
and spooked the Silly-Yak,
who sent the lady spinning
with a tinkle and a thwack.
The lady in the chandelier,
she dropped the golden boot
that fell into the fish tank
and kicked the flying newt.
The newt went flying through the air,
and after it I dashed,
but then I lost my balance and . . .

. . . the elephant got
SMASHED."

Silence.
No one moved.

In the room
everything was quiet.

Then from a corner
came a voice . . .

The giant turned to see young Olive
sitting with the storm,
her arm around its shoulder –
she *was* trying to keep it *warm*.

"This storm is not to blame," she said.
"I started all this mess,
with my sighing and my crying
and my ouchy grouchiness."

"The afternoon was boring,
there was nothing much to do,
so Grub and I, we ran upstairs
to play a game with you.

"The door was locked, and when we knocked
you grumbled, 'GO AWAY'.
So in a fit I made a wish
for stormy clouds all day."

"You mustn't leave forever.
We'll help you mend the elephant,
we'll mend it all together."

"Yes, *we*'ll mend it all together,"
said the giant. "My, oh my!

"And *when we*'re done we'll take the sun
and pop him in the sky.

3

"For tea we'll have a barbecue
and afterwards we'll play.

4

"By jumping round in puddles,
we can muddle through the day."

So it ended with a "YIPPEE!"
and a "LOOK OUT!" and a SPLASH!
And here comes Father Giant
with a smile in his moustache.

For Sonny

(t)

templar publishing

A TEMPLAR BOOK

First published in the UK in 2017 by Templar Publishing,
an imprint of Kings Road Publishing, part of the Bonnier Publishing Group,
The Plaza, 535 King's Road, London, SW10 0SZ
www.bonnierpublishing.com

1 3 5 7 9 10 8 6 4 2

ISBN 978-1-78370-773-7

This book was typeset in GlassLight
The illustrations were drawn in pen and ink
and coloured digitally

Designed by Genevieve Webster
Edited by Katie Haworth

Printed in China